For my mother and her father
— MTV

To my first born, we haven't met yet but I love
you already. Thanks for giving me a taste of
parenthood so I can better understand the
grandfather and mother in this story. Thank you
also for not doing too many somersaults in my
belly so I managed to finish this book.
— VN

Special thanks to Mạ, Cậu Chở, Dì Hạnh, and Zeinab for sharing their
stories; and to Anh Dũng, Thuyền, Kathryn, and Mary for assisting with
the research.

Library of Congress Cataloging-in-Publication Data available
ISBN 978-1-338-30589-0 • 10 9 8 7 6 5 4 3 2      21 22 23 24 25
Printed in the U.S.A.   88 • First edition, May 2021
The publisher would like to thank Vee B. Sotelo for her personal insight.
The text type was set in Volkorn. The display type was set in Stylish.
The book was printed on 140 gsm Golden Sun woodfree and bound by
RR Donnelley & Sons. Production was overseen by Catherine Weening.
Manufacturing was supervised by Shannon Rice. The book was art directed
by Patti Ann Harris, designed by Doan Buu, and edited by Celia Lee.

# wishes

By Mượn Thị Văn

Illustrations by Victo Ngai

Orchard Books
An Imprint of Scholastic Inc.
New York

The night wished it was quieter.

The bag wished
it was deeper.

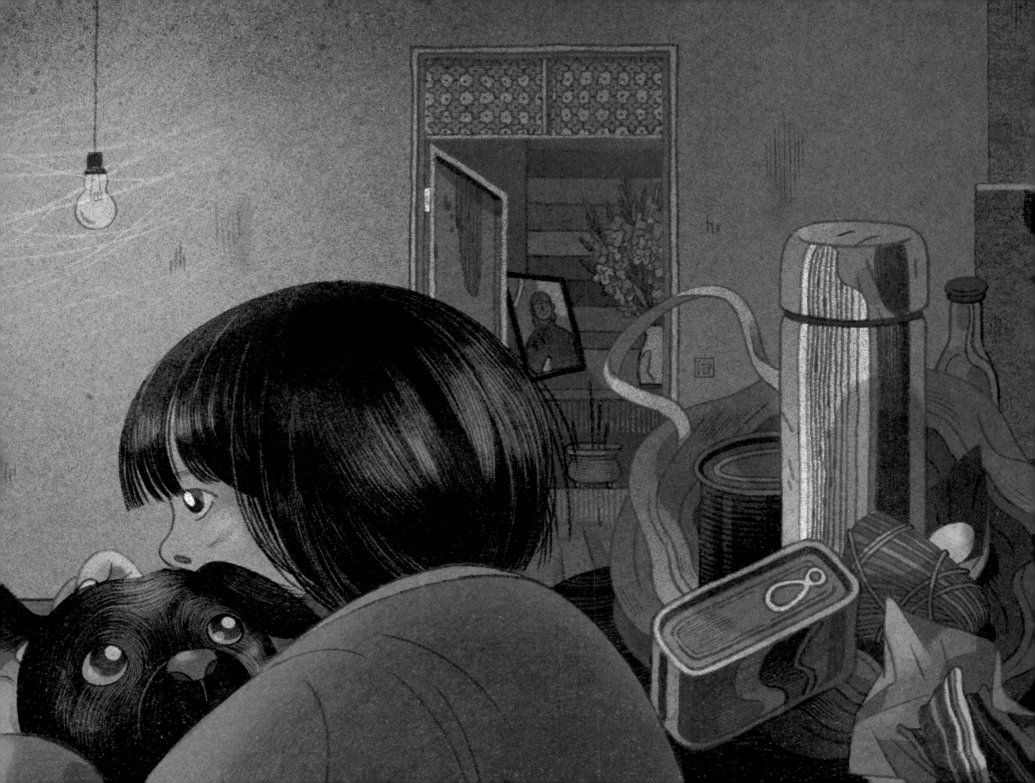

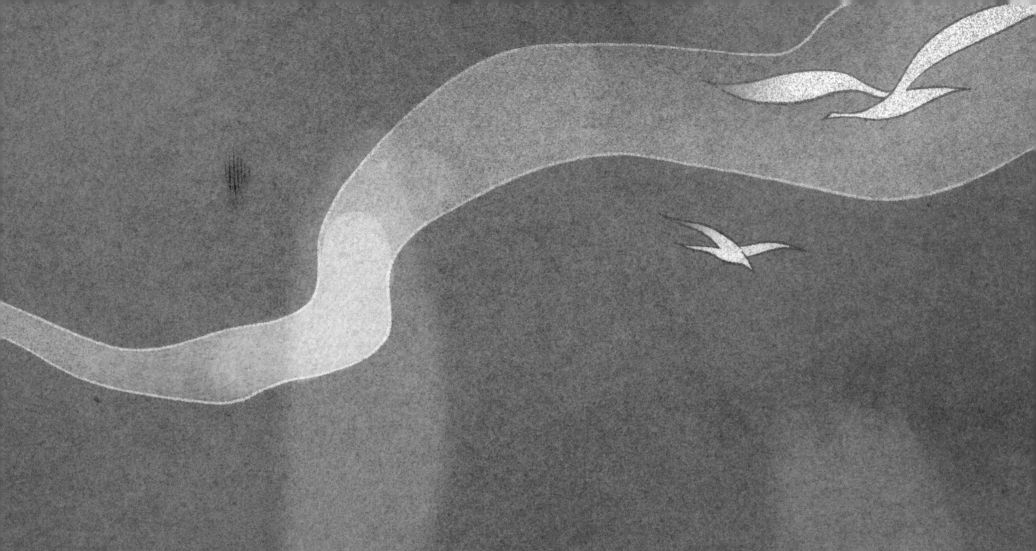

The light wished it was brighter.

The dream wished it was longer.

The clock wished
it was slower.

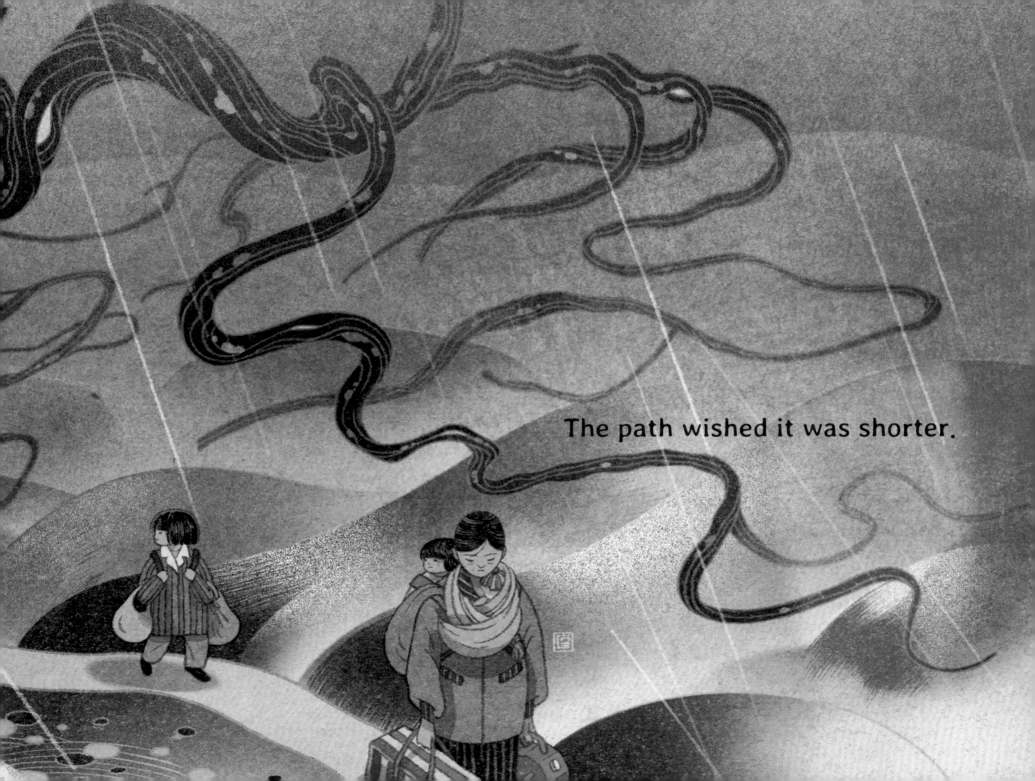

The path wished it was shorter.

The boat wished it was bigger.

The sea wished it was calmer.

The sun wished it was cooler.

The heart wished it was stronger.

The home wished it was closer.

And *I* wished . . .

I didn't have
to wish . . .

anymore.

# A Note from the Author

When I hear about secret escapes and border crossings, about family detentions and separations, about fear and loss but also about hope and new beginnings, I can't help but think of my family's own story and wonder: How long and how often will this story be told?

When I was born in 1980 in southern Việt Nam, my family had already been in hiding for several years. My father had served in the navy on the losing side of a long civil war that had ended a few years earlier. The new Vietnamese government was not kind to those who had previously opposed them. We were hiding so that my father would not be captured and imprisoned, where he might then die.

Soon after I arrived, my family quietly made our way back to our village. We stayed in a house near my grandfather's house, and my mother and her family began secret preparations for an oceanic voyage to Hong Kong. Almost no one knew we were leaving until the moment we left. On the night of our departure, every one of the twenty-two passengers aboard our boat left behind a child, a spouse, a parent, a grandparent, or a sibling. Some we never saw again, including my grandfather. We left streets and neighborhoods that were as familiar as the lines on our hands; we left customs and traditions that had been handed down for generations; we left communities that had shared in our joys and sorrows; we left our world, pursuing and hoping for a better one.

During our weekslong voyage at sea, we ran out of gas, we ran out of food, and we hit a storm so terrible it almost ended our journey and our lives. Some of our relatives lost their young children while making the same journey. Fortunately, everyone on our voyage survived and we even rescued four refugees stranded on the island of Hainan.

In the waters near Hong Kong, our boat was spotted by the local coast guard. We were eventually brought to a refugee camp where we stayed for almost a year before we found asylum and a new home in the United States.

More refugees are made every day, not only from local violence and persecution, but increasingly from catastrophic natural disasters and climate change effects. It is not always easy to decide whom to help and when.
But I think it is easy to open our hearts and to do what we can when we can.
Sometimes that means sharing what we don't need, whether it's food, clothing, or room.
Sometimes that means volunteering as a language tutor, a guide, or a driver.
Sometimes that means demonstrating to show support and solidarity, and sometimes that means petitioning to change laws and policies.
Sometimes doing what we can just means saying, "Hello."
I wish only for a safer, kinder, fairer, and more beautiful world.
I hope you'll join me in this wish. Together, we can make it come true.

— Mượn Thị Văn

# A Note from the Artist

Mượn's simple manuscript moved me immediately the first time I read it. There are only seventy-five words in total, yet a substantial amount of story and emotion are packed in between the lines. I am reminded of the six words of fiction often attributed to Ernest Hemingway: "For sale: baby shoes, never worn." The restraint and omission make the story all the more powerful and inspired my illustrative approach.

The narration told through inanimate objects especially affected me. The passivity amplifies the little choices individuals have in times of great change and turmoil. The third person perspective speaks to the universality of wishing for hope in a sea of helplessness, relatable to anyone who has to leave their home in search for a better life. This is why we decided to include an image on the outer case featuring not only our protagonist, but also refugees from other spaces and times.

As an artist working on this book, the biggest challenge for me is to also exercise restraint, to translate the emotions as honestly as I can, without the bright colors, elaborate compositions, or other stylizations and embellishments behind which one can hide many insecurities. Instead, I have observed the way afternoon sunlight dances across my apartment walls, softening the edges of objects — not unlike the hazy and fleeting feeling of a memory itself. I have also revisited old photos from my childhood, and borrowed some of the cracks, dents, and peeling paints from my grandmother's house as I want to glorify these imperfections since they are what give tactility and temperature to the idea of home.

— Victo Ngai